MOTHER HUBBARD'S CHRISTMAS

BY JOHN O'BRIEN

Boyds Mills Press

To Esther O'Brien,
that mother of mine,
I dedicate this book
—J.O.B.

Copyright © 1996 by John O'Brien

Published by Caroline House
Boyds Mills Press, Inc.
A Highlights Company
815 Church Street
Honesdale, Pennsylvania 18431
Printed in Mexico
Publisher Cataloging-in-Publication Data
O'Brien, John.
    Mother Hubbard's Christmas / by John O'Brien.—1st ed.
[32]p. : col. ill. ; cm.
Summary : The author gives his own holiday twist to the traditional Mother Goose rhyme.
ISBN 1-56397-139-9
1. Christmas—Fiction—Juvenile literature. [1. Christmas—Fiction.]
I. Title.
    [E]—dc20   1996   AC   CIP
Library of Congress Catalog Card Number 95-83169

First edition, 1996
Book designed by John O'Brien
The text of this book is set in 24-point Caslon Antique
The illustrations are done in pen and ink, dyes, and watercolors.

10 9 8 7 6 5 4 3 2 1

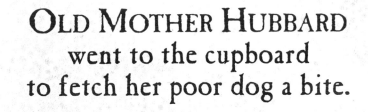

OLD MOTHER HUBBARD
went to the cupboard
to fetch her poor dog a bite.

But when she came there,
the cupboard was bare,
so the dog sang "Silent Night."

She went to the woods
to chop him a tree.

But when she got home,
he sawed it in three.

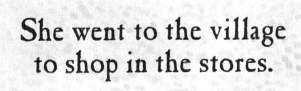

She went to the village
to shop in the stores.

But when she came back,
he locked all the doors.

She went to the driveway
to shovel a path.

But when she came back,
he was taking a bath.

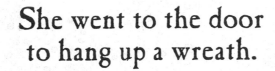

She went to the door
to hang up a wreath.

But when she came back,
he was brushing his teeth.

She climbed up the ladder
to light up the house.

But when she came down,
he was holding a mouse.

She went to the attic
to dig out his skates.

But when she came back,
he was juggling plates.

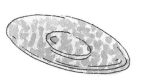

She went to the stove
to cook him a roast.

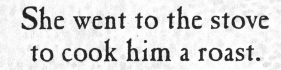

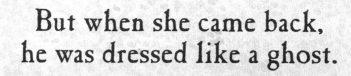

But when she came back,
he was dressed like a ghost.

She went to the piano
to play him a carol.

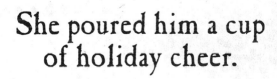

She poured him a cup
of holiday cheer.

But when she looked up,
he was riding a deer.

She went up the stairs
to get ready for bed.

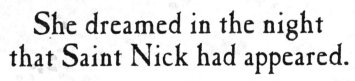

She dreamed in the night
that Saint Nick had appeared.

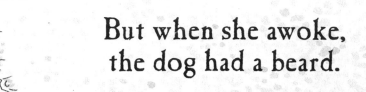

But when she awoke,
the dog had a beard.

She gave him a gift
and got one of her own.

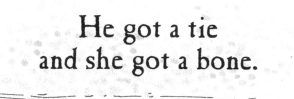

He got a tie
and she got a bone.

She went to the table,
and there she did sup...

On a holiday feast
the dog had cooked up.

The dame made a curtsy.
The dog made a bow.
The dame said, "Your servant."
And the dog said, "Ho! Ho! Ho!"